EASY COME EASY DOUGH

RAISED AND GLAZED COZY MYSTERIES,
BOOK 17

EMMA AINSLEY

SUMMER PRESCOTT BOOKS PUBLISHING

CHAPTER ONE

Maggie Sharpe checked the display case fifteen minutes before opening. She had filled the case with cake donuts frosted in bright colors, having felt the need to brighten the world a little bit. They were in the worst heat of the summer and outside, the warm sun baked the Ozark mountains that loomed above the small town of Dogwood Mountain, Missouri.

"Looks like the Easter bunny hit the display case overnight," Ruby Cobb, Maggie's best friend and business partner, observed. Normally there well before five in the morning, Ruby had arrived for work just before seven. As the newly elected Dogwood Mountain City Council member, Ruby had attended a late night event the night before and needed a little extra time to sleep in.

"I thought we might need some bright colors in the case this morning," Maggie said with a shrug.

"You have some news, don't you?" Ruby leaned her elbow on the case and blocked the way for Maggie to pass. "You have to tell me."

With a smile and a bit of a struggle, Maggie slipped past her and headed straight for the kitchen. "I have no idea what you're talking about." She returned with another tray of bright blue cupcakes.

"Are they coming today? Is it today?" In her fifties, Ruby was well beyond bouncing where she stood, but she clapped her hands gleefully to make up for it.

"Good morning, Aunt Ruby," Bradley Sharpe's voice boomed behind her. Maggie's only child was as close to Ruby as he might have been to Maggie's own biological sister. He turned his wiggling son, Wyatt, around and passed him straight into Ruby's waiting arms.

"I can't believe you're here," Ruby said. She cuddled the small boy against her. Wyatt noticed the blue cupcakes and leaned toward them. Maggie scooped him from Ruby's arm while her son hugged her best friend. "So, does this mean you're out of the Navy?"

Bradley released her and nodded his head. "I am

officially out," he said. "And I have my first job interview in Joplin in the morning."

"Oh, does that mean you need someone to watch this young man in the morning?" Ruby asked.

"We're watching him here," Maggie answered. "I plan to set his portable crib up in the office while we work. He should sleep for part of the morning but there will be enough of us here to keep a close eye on him."

"Josie and Naomi will both be here," Ruby said. "I want to cross train them on opening the store."

Maggie and Ruby had gone through several potential employees, but after a couple of prospects they both thought were solid additions to the team, Josie and Naomi had both emerged as the right fit. Josie was the younger of the pair. She worked part time while her husband managed their two small kids at home.

Naomi was recently divorced and wanted full-time work. She was Maggie's favorite for the potential position of supervisor. Myra Sawyer Macklin, the default manager of the donut shop, was growing more and more burdened each day as her pregnancy wore on.

"Good," Maggie said. "We will make sure Mr. Wyatt here is carefully watched."

"And if these women are all too busy with their donuts and their cinnamon rolls and coffees, just us guys will hang out together," Orson Hawley said. As another beloved member of the Dogwood Donuts' staff, the fact that he was growing older and slowing down at the shop only meant that a lot of his time was spent at the Old Timer's table instead of behind the counter.

Wyatt smiled and held his arms out. "Come here, big guy," Orson said to the small boy. "You come on over here with Papa Orson and have your breakfast."

"That makes me very happy," Maggie whispered when Orson walked away. Eventually, he planned to be the backup morning babysitter for Myra's new baby. He'd said that it was the least he could do for Myra and her police officer husband, Brooks Macklin. When the couple married, they'd made room in their new home for Orson to live out the rest of his days in a private apartment.

"Tell me about this job interview." Ruby turned back to Bradley. "What number is this? Four?"

"It's my fifth interview, but the first one in person," Bradley said. Since his terminal leave in the Navy began, he had made use of the internet to conduct most of his job interviews. Maggie had been surprised to find the number of interviewers who preferred a remote interview nowadays.

"Where is this job?" Ruby asked.

"It's at a security company called Armored Shield," he said. "My job would be to help develop software and software upgrades for the integrated security systems for residential and business accounts."

"Is this a job you want to do?" Ruby asked.

"It is actually right along the lines of what I want," he said. "And the best part is that half the time I can work from home. I'm really hoping that this interview goes well."

"We're all hoping that it goes well for you," Maggie said. "Otherwise, I may have to put you to work in the donut food truck."

"Are you still taking the truck to the Summer Fair in Hunter Springs over the weekend?" Orson asked from across the dining room.

"I am." Maggie was grateful for the chance to take the food truck out of the donut shop parking lot for once. The truck hadn't gotten a lot of use lately and she hated to think that purchasing it was nothing but a waste of time and money.

"It does seem like a stretch to call the fair a 'summer fair,'" Ruby said. "It's already September."

"Just the beginning of September," Orson argued. "Summer isn't officially over for another couple of weeks."

"I know," Ruby said. "But generally, September events are usually characterized as autumn events."

"Anyway," Maggie interjected. "I have a feeling this weekend in Hunter Springs is going to be a big deal for us. Word of mouth is one of the very best ways to gain more customers. If people see us there and like what we have to offer, I think it could really make a difference for us overall. I'm excited about it."

"Well then, I am too," Ruby agreed. "Let's make this a weekend to remember."

"Everything you two seem to do is memorable." Orson grinned at the women and then turned to his friends. He snickered and in a not so quiet whisper, he added, "and that's not always a good thing."

CHAPTER TWO

Maggie peered through the gap between the office door and the doorjamb at the small boy sleeping in the portable crib. She listened for a moment and watched as he cuddled the tiny plush bear in his arms. Wyatt sighed and cuddled the bear closer. Maggie smiled and exhaled slowly. She loved the fact that the small boy would now be so much closer to her.

"Is he still sleeping?" Ruby asked her when she returned to the kitchen. She kept her voice lower than normal as she worked.

"He's cuddling his bear and sleeping soundly," Maggie said. She checked the automatic donut machines and added more batter to each of the hoppers. While the machines were running, she gathered the supplies from the storeroom and the cooler for a large batch of frosting.

She blended the butter and the powdered sugar with milk and set the white frosting aside. She carefully measured out four portions and colored them with the same bright colors she'd used the day before. This time, however, Maggie mixed in flavoring for each color. She added blueberry to the blue colored frosting, cherry flavoring to the pink frosting, lemon to the bright yellow frosting, and then stood back and stared at the last bucket she had mixed with the light green tint.

"Ruby," Maggie whispered. "Should I do mint or lime for the light green?"

"Key lime," Ruby said.

"Oh, yeah. Great idea," Maggie said. She ran to the storeroom for more supplies. She almost giggled at the thought of a more tropical flavor in the case. With Wyatt sleeping in the office and her son off at a job interview, Maggie felt unusually buoyant.

Ten minutes later, she presented a cooled key lime frosted donut to Ruby, who stood at the prep table assembling boxed lunches for the afternoon.

"What do you think?" she asked when her best friend took a bite.

"I think we ought to have key lime donuts more often," she said. She moved to the baker's table and sampled each of the other varieties. "I think we need to figure out how to include the flavor into the donut batter. And maybe add an orange donut, too. This ought to be a new line we advertise and include in the daily menu."

"Really? You think so?" Maggie asked.

"Absolutely," Ruby said. "These are classic flavors, and I would almost bet we will sell out of the cake donuts faster and faster each day. We can still add the seasonal and holiday flavors, too. But let's have Myra make a poster for the counter and put an ad in the paper about the new 'happy flavors' in our cake donuts."

"'Happy flavors,'" Maggie said plainly.

"Well, we can come up with a better name for them, but you get the point," Ruby said.

She laughed and began searching her phone for cake donut flavor mixes. She had to rely on her phone while the baby slept in her office. "Oh, I have a text from Bradley."

"Is everything okay?" Ruby asked.

Maggie pulled the text up on her screen. "He asked about the baby," she said and typed a quick answer. "And he said that the interviewer didn't show up. He's been calling for a new time, but can't get anyone to answer."

"The manager didn't show up to meet with him?" she asked. "Where were they supposed to meet?"

"I thought they were meeting at the office, but I could be wrong," Maggie said. She texted Bradley the question quickly and waited for the reply. "He said they had plans to meet at some café with a community office space."

"That's really weird," Ruby said. "Why wouldn't they meet at their own office? Was this some sort of a test?"

"I don't know what kind of test it would be, but I sure hope not," Maggie said. "Because if it was, my son just failed it."

A tiny cry from the office distracted her from her conversation with Ruby. She put up her finger and quietly walked toward the office. She peeked in the doorway and smiled when she spotted Wyatt sitting up in his portable crib and pointed his finger at her. He raised his hands high above his head.

"Good morning, little man," Maggie said. She pushed the door open and smiled. Wyatt danced in place in excitement. "Oh, you are getting bigger!" She pulled him up to her chest and kissed him on top of the head.

"Are we awake?" Ruby peeked in and asked.

"Oh, I think he's wide awake," Maggie said. "Maybe we ought to get this guy some breakfast."

"On it," Ruby said. She headed for the cooler and returned with the makings for a first class omelet.

"Do you really think he's going to eat all of that?" Maggie asked.

Ruby shrugged. "What's the point of having an executive chef as a great-aunt if you don't get treated to a gourmet meal every once in a while?"

"I'm going to run to the restroom and change him fast," Maggie said while Ruby set about making the eggs. "I'll let Naomi know that I need her to come back here and take over for me. Can you fill her in on the plans for the cake donuts?"

"I will," Ruby promised. "But I think you need to come up with a better name for them than just the 'colorful cake donuts.' If we're going to advertise these, we need a catchy name."

"I'll work on it, but remember for today just the icing is flavored." She settled Wyatt on her hip and headed for the employee restroom with the backpack Bradley had packed for him.

When she returned, Ruby was spooning his food onto a small plate. She had poured some milk for him and placed both on a tray for Maggie, along with a small bowl of soft fruits.

"I'll follow you out to the booth," Ruby said. Maggie headed through the swinging kitchen door with the baby on her hip. He waved the second he spotted Orson at the Old Timer's table.

"Hey there, buddy." Orson waved back. Maggie grabbed a wooden highchair and carried it with her free hand to the booth on the far side of the counter. She set it down and carefully placed Wyatt inside.

Ruby set the tray on the table and reached down to secure him with the safety belt. Immediately, Wyatt began drumming the table with his tiny hands. "Hold on just a minute, sir," Ruby said. She picked up the spoon and cut a piece of the omelet off and fed him. "Very good taste, Mr. Wyatt." When she was finished, she handed the spoon off to Maggie. "Here you are, Mimi. I just wanted to feed him one bite."

"Ruby, if you want to feed him, I'll head back into the kitchen and work with Naomi."

"No, that's fine," Ruby said. "I need to work on the boxed lunches, anyway. You go on and enjoy breakfast with this distinct gentleman." She tousled Wyatt's thick hair and headed back to the kitchen.

"Excuse me, miss?" An older woman rose up from her seat near the window. "Why isn't that dish on the menu? I would like an omelet."

Maggie looked up from where she was seated. "Oh, we don't serve omelets," she said.

The woman cleared her throat. "Then why are you sitting there with an omelet on your plate?" she asked.

"Ma'am," Ruby stopped halfway to the kitchen. "I just made that for the baby."

"That's not fair," the woman said.

"Please sit down, Ellen," the man seated across from her said in a loud whisper.

"I'm Maggie, the owner of this place," she said. "This is my grandson, and we're feeding him eggs rather than just donuts or another pastry. Eggs aren't on the menu here. I apologize for the confusion."

The woman opened her mouth to speak, but stopped when the man across from her cleared his throat again. Maggie turned her attention back to Wyatt. "I think someone needs a nap," she whispered. "What do you think?"

CHAPTER THREE

Bradley arrived around one to pick up Wyatt and return to Maggie's house for another internet search. He had tried over and over to reach the man he had been set to meet with, but there was no response and no answer on the man's phone.

When she got home at last, Maggie suggested that Bradley call the main number to the company and ask for another interview. When he did, he inquired about the man he was set to meet with, only to be placed on hold and eventually disconnected.

"Do you want to come and hang out with me at the food truck over the weekend?" Maggie asked. "Wyatt can come as well, or maybe we can see if Myra wants to hang out with him for a little while."

"I'd better ask Orson first," Bradley said. "He

informed me that I am to ask him to babysit first before anyone else."

"Well, maybe you ought to give Orson a call and see if he's busy on Saturday," Maggie suggested.

"Maybe that can be my new job, Mom," Bradley said ruefully. "I can park the food truck in Hunter Springs and sell donuts instead of working in tech."

Maggie laughed nervously and set a basket of Wyatt's laundry on the kitchen table and began folding things. She wanted to ask Bradley if his plan to stick around the Ozarks would change if he couldn't find the job he wanted. After all, Kansas City, where his father lived, was something of a tech destination. Would he take Wyatt and head north instead of remaining close to Dogwood Mountain?

"I just thought you might like to come and see what the food truck is all about," she said. "I mean, to be honest, Bradley, one day my part of the donut shop and this house will be yours."

Her son looked up and eyed her carefully. "What are you talking about, Mom?" he asked. He sounded annoyed.

"Unless you don't want it, someday when I'm too old to run this any longer, it will all go to you and Wyatt."

"It will?" he asked. He bounced Wyatt on his knee.

Maggie shrugged. "Who else is going to take over?"

"Good point," he said.

A little while later, Maggie spooned a few spaghetti noodles into a small bowl and topped it with marinara sauce. She then used a fork to smash the noodles into smaller pieces and set the bowl on the table next to the highchair.

Bradley set Wyatt in his chair and straightened up to answer his phone. "I have to take this, Mom," he announced and headed out the back door.

"I guess you are stuck with your Mimi feeding you again," Maggie said.

"Mimi," Wyatt said in response.

Maggie nearly dropped the spoon in her hand. "What did you just say?" she asked. Wyatt said nothing more, but opened his mouth for another bite. She knew it was nothing more than baby babble, but she wouldn't dwell on that part.

"Can you say Mimi?" Maggie asked between bites.

Wyatt, of course, said nothing. He did, however, quickly devour about half of the spaghetti. Maggie rose to refill his milk when Bradley walked back through the back door followed by Brett Mission, Dogwood Mountain Chief of Police and Maggie's boyfriend.

"What's going on?" she asked. Her son's face appeared ashen.

"We need to talk for a moment," Brett said. Bradley sat down at the table and tossed his phone across the surface.

"Bradley," Maggie asked slowly. "What's the matter?"

"William Anderson was found dead this afternoon," Brett announced.

Bradley dropped his head into his hands and stared at the surface of the table.

"Am I supposed to know who that is?" Maggie asked. She'd never heard the name before.

"He's talking about the man I was supposed to meet today for an interview," Bradley said, eyeing Brett carefully.

"I told you; I only have a few questions to ask you," Brett said.

"I'm sorry, man," Bradley said. "I've been down this road before, Chief. Only last time I didn't have a little boy here to take care of. I'm not going to go to jail over something I didn't do."

"As far as I can tell, nobody thinks that you did

anything," Brett said. "If they did, they wouldn't rely on me to ask you a few questions instead of sending their own investigators."

"Who are you talking about?" Maggie asked.

"The Joplin police, for one," Brett said. "As well as the county sheriff, possibly the state police. Any one of them would have come down here if they thought of this as more than a formality."

"Alright," Bradley said. "What do you want to ask me?"

"Tell me about what happened this morning," Brett said.

"I woke up around five and got my son ready for my mom to take him to work with her," Bradley said.

"Mom left with Wyatt right before six. I showered and left for Joplin before seven."

"When was your interview scheduled?"

"Eight-thirty," Bradley said.

"Did you stop anywhere else when you got to Joplin? Or anywhere in between?" Brett asked.

Bradley thought for a moment. "I was tired from not getting much sleep, so I grabbed a coffee when I got into town," he said. "I went to a chain coffee shop right when I pulled into town off the highway."

"Do you have any idea what time that was?" Brett asked.

"Not off the top of my head, but I can find out." Bradley pulled out his phone and spent a half a minute scrolling through information on the screen. When he was finished, he turned the screen to Brett. "There. It was about four minutes after eight when I paid at the drive-thru. I must have been there for a few minutes before that, though."

"What is that?" Maggie asked, pointing at the screen.

"Oh, I paid for my coffee with an app on my phone," Bradley said. "And this is the receipt."

"Can you take a shot of that screen and send it to my phone?" Brett asked.

"Sure, if you can give me the number," Bradley said.

Brett rattled off his cell phone number and waited for the text to hit his phone. He excused himself outside and returned a few moments later. Maggie wiped Wyatt's face and put him down for a nap while Brett was outside her back door. He returned when Maggie walked back into the kitchen.

"Alright, Bradley," Brett said. "I've spoken with the Joplin Police Department and sent the information you gave me their way. Right now, they appear to be satisfied. They've not asked for further information at this time. I know what you're worried about, and I'd love to tell you not to worry about anything, but I don't think I can guarantee without a doubt that the police won't want to speak to you again. I can't make that promise outright, but I feel comfortable telling you that I feel about ninety-five percent sure you have nothing to worry about."

"That's a relief," Bradley said, and Maggie hoped it was true.

CHAPTER FOUR

Maggie checked in at the donut shop first thing the following morning. Ruby was already in the kitchen and Naomi, the new full-time employee, was at the baker's table. Maggie smiled when she saw the woman hunched over and rolling out the cinnamon roll dough with gusto.

"How are things going here this morning?" she asked when she walked into the storeroom for an extra tub of frosting.

"Good," Ruby said. "Actually, quite excellent." She nodded toward the baker's table.

"How are you this morning, Naomi?" Maggie asked.

"Oh, good morning, Maggie," Naomi said. "I'm right as rain. And yourself?"

"I'm great." Maggie grinned. "I'd better get on the road to Hunter Springs, though. The food truck awaits."

"Have fun," Ruby called after her.

Maggie waved and headed back to her car. She turned up her radio and sang along as she drove through town and then onto the highway to Hunter Springs. The fair was set to open at nine, so she wasn't too worried about an early morning arrival. At seven, she had plenty of time to get the food truck ready and the mini donut machine producing fresh donuts for a nine o'clock opening.

Maggie turned off the highway and headed downtown. She passed the site of the old diner where she had met Flo Johnson for the first time. Flo now ran her own food truck under the sign at the far end of the donut shop parking lot.

Cars packed the downtown area. Maggie followed the signs for the vendors' parking lot and found an empty space close to the entrance. She watched as other vendors carried large containers of merchandise or other goods through the gates and down the long road toward their booths or storefronts.

She was grateful that the only thing she had to carry to the food truck was a small tub of frosting. The food truck was parked on a side street right off of the main road. She didn't have far to walk. When she parked the truck with Ruby a few days before, their truck was the only one parked on the side street. She was surprised to see a coffee truck, three other food trucks, and a funnel cake stand.

Ten minutes after she opened the door, the mini donut machine was heating up and the cinnamon roll dough was rising in the warming drawer under the cabinet. Maggie set to work rolling out the scone dough she had left in the food truck refrigerator the night before. She decided to make the menu fairly basic for the fair. She kept the coffee syrups to about a half dozen for lattes and cappuccinos. The scone flavors were similar to the coffee syrup flavors, so they'd match well.

She added the cinnamon rolls, glazed donuts in either chocolate or vanilla, and a single jelly-filled Bismarck dusted with confectioner's sugar.

One hour after she arrived at the food truck, Maggie brewed a simple pot of coffee for herself and took a seat at the small table in the back of the truck. Myra had offered to come around ten and relieve her, but Maggie told her not to worry about it. She had hoped for the fair to be a small boost of revenue for the month of September. But the chance that the fair would be that busy was unlikely. Hunter Springs was larger in area and population than Dogwood Mountain, but with a minor coffee chain drive-thru on Main Street, she wondered if the town would support a donut shop. The fair provided some novelty, at least temporarily. She'd hoped it would, anyway.

At ten minutes before nine, Maggie stepped out of the food truck and surveyed the front of the truck. She wanted to make sure to represent the donut shop well, essentially to put the best face forward of the business. Hopefully, the food truck would draw business to Dogwood Mountain as well.

Maggie waved at the coffee truck across from her. She noticed the sign for the first time. The coffee truck was actually an outreach for a local church. She squinted to read the menu from where she stood. She was halfway pleased to see the limited selection offered. The coffee shop offered basic black coffee with a variety of cream flavors.

Immediately, she felt bad and decided to order a cup from the church group before the end of the day. She stepped back up into the food truck and unlatched the order and delivery windows. She expected to have a few minutes before any customers showed up and decided to pop her phone out of her pocket. She searched for the name of the church on the coffee truck across the road from her and read a little about their mission and outreach.

She looked up when she heard a tap on the glass. "Uh, are you open?" Maggie looked into the face of a young woman holding the hand of a small child.

"Oh, I'm sorry," she said. "I am open. What can I get you?"

"I'll take a dozen chocolate mini donuts and a cinnamon latte."

Maggie nodded and totaled the order. She went to work on the latte and pulled a dozen mini donuts from the warming drawer. When she returned to the window with the order, she was shocked to see a line of people had formed behind the woman.

Over the next two hours, the line continued to wax and wane. Never less than five people in line, the amount swelled to over ten people waiting to order coffee and donuts while she worked constantly to fill the orders.

By ten in the morning, Maggie's feet ached and her lower back spasmed off and on. When she had a brief break, she mixed up the next batch of batter for the mini donut machine. She ran the machine in steps. As soon as a batch was finished, she sprinkled it with cinnamon and sugar or powdered sugar and delivered it to a waiting customer.

At noon, Maggie called the donut shop in Dogwood Mountain and begged for more supplies. She was out of cinnamon rolls and scones, and her coffee supplies were running low. She asked for Jake or Naomi to bring two more large bags of donut mix for the mini donut machine. When she returned to the order window, the line outside had grown by another five customers.

Maggie worked through the line and placed her "be back in five minutes" sign in the order window just long enough to use the restroom.

Once more, she was so grateful she had purchased a food truck with its own bathroom on board. She emerged in less than three minutes and found another ten people waiting outside. She removed the sign, opened the window, and took more orders.

Ruby herself arrived thirty minutes later. "I come bearing gifts," she announced and hefted the first fifty-pound bag of mix into the back door. Bradley stepped inside a moment later with two more bags while Ruby returned to her truck. She had carried a large tote with chilled cinnamon roll dough inside. Bradley ran back to the truck for two trays of pre-made scones.

"Where is Wyatt?" Maggie asked Bradley when he returned.

"Orson has him for a couple of hours," he said. "I drove here so I could help you out this afternoon for a little while."

"And I'm here to help you as well," Ruby said. "Why don't you go and get some lunch somewhere while Bradley and I run the truck?"

"Are you sure? I planned to close up by three," Maggie said.

"I don't know about that," Ruby said. "From these crowds, we might be here for a little while."

"Yeah, Mom," Bradley said. "Go on and get out of here. We've got this."

CHAPTER FIVE

Maggie left her son and her best friend in the food truck and set out to walk around the fair. She headed for the main road through the booths. She passed another small cluster of food trucks and stopped to order a walking taco and a sweet tea.

While she waited for the order, she was approached by a smiling man in a navy blue suit. "Pardon me," the man said. "Are you the person running the donut shop food truck down on Second Street?"

"I am," Maggie said suspiciously.

"Well, welcome to Hunter Springs," he said. "Allow me to introduce myself. John Huffy, Mayor of Hunter Springs. I believe you all are from Dogwood Mountain?"

"Yes, that's right," Maggie said. She accepted his extended hand and shook it.

"Forgive me for being so forward, but are you Ruby Cobb, or maybe Myra? I looked into the donut shop online a little while ago," Mayor Huffy said. "You have quite a lot of business going right now."

"Actually, my name is Maggie Sharpe," she said.

"Oh! You're the owner," he said. His eyes widened, and he took her hand in his once again.

Maggie smiled. "I am, although Ruby Cobb owns a part of the business," she said. "She's my business partner."

"Well, I have to tell you, we were so excited to see your name on the fair manifest," he said. "Everyone of us at city hall has driven to Dogwood Mountain to pick up an order of donuts and coffee for a morning meeting."

"I thought you had a coffee shop here," Maggie said without thinking.

"We do," the mayor said. "It's a chain coffee shop. A lot of our high schoolers hang out in the parking lot after school."

"Oh, I see," she said. Her order was ready, and she stepped up to take it. "It was nice to meet you."

"Wait, Mrs. Sharpe," he said.

"It's Ms., but call me Maggie."

"Okay, Maggie," he said. "I hope you'll consider coming back with your food truck quite often. I mean, I would love it if you decided to speak to one of our local real estate agents about some commercial space. But I'm sure that's a lot to hope for."

Maggie looked longingly at the warm Mexican food in her hands. Her stomach growled and her mouth watered. "I was just speaking to Ruby and my son about seeing if we can park the food truck in Hunter Springs over the next few weekends."

"Oh, really?" The mayor was practically giddy. "We have a business park you can check out. It's right at the end of Main Street near the bank. It's a very popular spot."

"I'll have to check it out," Maggie replied with a smile. She took a step away and hoped the mayor got the message that she was ready to head off to enjoy her lunch.

"I tell you what," he said and reached into his back pocket for his wallet. He fished out a business card. "You call me on Monday morning, and we'll work out a great deal for the lot rent. I might even be able to swing a couple of weekends for free."

Maggie took the card and turned it over in her hand. She held tightly to her food with the other hand. "Mayor, why would you do that?" she asked. "I mean, don't get me wrong. I would be very grateful for any discounts or help. But why would the city want to give us a break on the lot rent? Don't you benefit from the rent?"

"We actually make much more money from the sales tax outside businesses collect when they visit," he said. "I was just elected to my second term as mayor of this town. My number one focus and campaign promise was to bring new business to Hunter Springs. Now, I don't want you to think we're trying to pull you out of Dogwood Mountain. Your mayor, Jason Savino, is a friend of mine."

"Ruby was just elected to the city council, too," Maggie offered.

"Well, see? That's even more of a reason to make this point." The mayor laughed. "I don't want to pull you away from your hometown, but if you're considering an expansion, I hope you give us some consideration. Your business is extremely popular here. I would love for there to be a Hunter Springs Donut Shop."

"You make a very compelling case, Mayor," Maggie said. "It was very nice to meet you. Please make sure you stop by in the morning. I'll be sure to have a complimentary coffee and pastry for you."

She picked up her sweet tea and left him with

another smile and a nod and headed back toward the food truck. Her walking taco had become cold. "Thank goodness for the small microwave in the food truck," she thought. When the food truck was back in her view, she could see the line out front had not thinned at all.

"Sorry that took so long," Maggie said when she opened the door and climbed back into the food truck. Her first move was to reheat the taco in the microwave. "I'll eat really fast and relieve you two."

"I think I'm going to hang out for the rest of the day," Bradley announced.

"Are you sure?" Maggie asked. "You had said something about it before, but what about Wyatt?"

"Orson is fine with him right now," Bradley said. "I just checked in on them."

"And I'm going to run by and snatch him up when I get back," Ruby said. "I think he'd enjoy a little time out on the farm with me."

"We shouldn't be here for more than another couple of hours," Maggie said.

"I don't know, Mom," Bradley said. "I think if we can hold out for a few more hours, we ought to keep the truck open for as long as we still have supplies. Even if we get down to fresh mini donuts and coffee, we ought to keep the lights on as long as the customers are lined up."

"I don't want to be here too late," Maggie said. She pulled her taco from the microwave and sat down to eat. "I still have prep work for tomorrow to get to this evening. And after today, I think I better come a little more prepared."

"I think we should add a few more items to the menu for tomorrow," Bradley said. "I mean, clearly the glazed donuts and cinnamon rolls outsell the jelly-filled donuts. And the mini donut varieties outdo everything."

"Okay, Boy Wonder," Ruby teased. "Do you think you can manage this all by yourself?"

Bradley shrugged his shoulders slightly and nodded his head. "I've watched Mom a bunch of times, and you just taught me how to run the mini donut maker. I certainly think I can figure out an iPad for sales."

"You know, the mayor of Hunter Springs just stopped me in front of The Taco Hut. And he was sure dropping hints about the possibility of us parking the food truck here on the weekends. He even offered me free rent."

"Really?" Ruby sounded surprised. "Do you think

the mayor just likes donuts, or could there be another motive?"

"Honestly," Maggie said. "I think he wants me to call a real estate agent and start viewing commercial properties right now."

"Does he want us to move here or open a second location here?" Bradley asked.

"A second location," Maggie said, loving his use of the word 'us'. "He will settle for the food truck on the weekends, though."

"So, maybe it's that he likes donuts too much," Ruby joked.

"Actually, he said that bringing in new business was a top campaign promise that won him the mayor's seat for a second term. He hopes to bring in more business and has watched how well we're doing over here. Plus, he said he loves our shop in Dogwood Mountain, too."

"What about the other coffee shop?" Bradley asked. As he spoke, he removed the hot donuts from the machine and sprinkled cinnamon and sugar all over them.

"That's the odd thing," Maggie said. "He spoke as if he preferred the thought of a locally owned business over a national chain."

"Okay, Mom," Bradley said. "I'm going to hang

around until we run out of everything. Let's just see how long we can hold out. You can head home and get ready for tomorrow if you want. I think I can handle this on my own tonight. Aunt Ruby has shown me a lot over the past couple of hours."

Maggie beamed and finally agreed. She loved how interested her son was.

CHAPTER SIX

"It's still busy." Bradley texted Maggie just after six. "I think I can hold out until seven, but after that, I'll probably be out of everything."

"And people are still showing up?" Maggie texted back. She had to wait a few moments before he answered. He sent along a photo of the street outside of the front of the food truck.

"The line is still about five people deep constantly."

Maggie prepared two extra batches of cinnamon roll dough. She worked on the scones while the cinnamon rolls were rising the first time. When the cinnamon rolls had risen, she punched the dough down and rolled it out thin. Then she spread real butter, brown sugar, cinnamon, and white sugar over the rolled out dough.

Starting at one end, Maggie carefully rolled the dough up and pinched the ends until all of it was pinched and sealed. She cut the cinnamon roll dough into one inch sections and placed them on a greased baking sheet. She placed the baking sheets in the cooler to flash freeze while she finished the scones and prepared them for the cooler.

When she was finished at the donut shop, Maggie locked everything up tight and stopped by her house on the way out to Ruby's to pick Wyatt up. She quickly changed her clothes and threw water on her face to freshen up.

Maggie dressed in a fresh pair of yoga pants from the dryer, put on a clean t-shirt, and headed out to her car. The air had cooled enough that she decided to run back inside and grab a light sweatshirt. She drove toward the edge of town and headed south. She passed the old bookstore that had once belonged to her friend Faylene and sighed.

As she drove around the front, Maggie noticed the lights on inside the bookstore. She pulled her car into the parking lot without thinking and walked up to the front doors. She could see right into the store through the windows, which had been covered with white butcher paper since Faylene moved out of state. Today, the paper had been removed.

A man with thick silver hair stood at the top of a ladder. His hand was inside one of the many light fixtures. Maggie raised her fist to bang on the glass but thought better of it. The last thing she wanted was to cause a terrible accident with the man falling to the ground below from the high ladder. She also didn't want to be responsible for his injuries.

Still, Maggie felt more than a little protective of the store. She decided to get back into her car and head out to Ruby's farm as planned. But before she could leave, the man on the ladder turned and spotted her staring in the window.

Maggie turned on her heels and headed quickly back to her car. She'd just reached her door when the front door to the bookstore scraped over the sidewalk. The man stood there gaping at her from the doorway.

"Is there something I can help you with?" he asked.

"No," Maggie said quickly. "I was just wondering who was here in Faylene's bookstore."

"This isn't her bookstore any longer," the man said. "And by all rights, you are trespassing."

"Did you buy it? Are you keeping it as a bookstore?"

"You ask a lot of questions," the man snapped.

"Well, Faylene is a friend of mine, and I didn't realize she'd officially sold the place."

"I don't care if she was a friend of the pope's. And what I do with this place is my business."

"Okay then. I didn't mean to be rude or cause trouble." Maggie turned to open her car door.

"Great, but you're still trespassing," the man said.

"What's your name?" Maggie asked.

"What's yours?"

Flustered, Maggie climbed inside her car. She started the engine with the man still staring her down. She pulled out of the parking space and headed for the road, but stopped in front of the bookstore. "I was really only wondering if someone was inside the store who didn't belong," she said after rolling down the window. "I didn't intend to trespass or to be rude. The woman who owned this before is a dear friend of mine."

"But you did trespass, and you were rude," he said. "I suppose you're expecting a thank you for looking out for my property, which is mine legally, by the way, but I won't be needing your busybody services any longer. I am no relation to the previous owner. In fact, I'm new to this town and will likely sell this property once I finish repairs. Good day, madam." The man walked back inside the door and stared at Maggie as he turned the lock.

Maggie drove straight to the farm and pulled her car to an abrupt stop. She met Ruby at the back door with a smiling and dirty Wyatt on her hip.

"What have you two been up to?" she asked. Wyatt kicked his legs in delight and hugged Ruby.

"Oh, we were just playing in the dirt," Ruby said. Dirt was smudged on her own face. "I was just about to clean him up."

"I can do that," Maggie offered. She held her arms out for her grandson. He leaned over and she carried him straight to the bathroom and washed up his face and hands.

"Are you going to fill me in on what's got you all in a tizzy?"

Maggie leveled her gaze on her best friend. "I stopped by the bookstore to see why there were lights burning inside and the man who was in there was a real jerk."

"What's his name?" Ruby asked.

Maggie shook her head. "I have no idea," she said. "He wouldn't tell me. He just said that he had purchased the bookstore and that he is not a relative of Faylene's."

"Well, that's not exactly a mark against him," Ruby said.

"True, but it still gave me a weird feeling," she said. "I hate the thought that we might have to put up with him on a regular basis in this town. He said he might just sell it, but who knows?"

"Maybe he'll do just that, and we won't have to worry about him at all," Ruby said. "I hope the bookstore remains, but we both know how that goes."

"Anyway, I think I'm going to take this big guy home and put him to bed," Maggie said. "His dad is going to be a little while yet, I'm afraid."

"It sounds like he's had quite the busy day," Ruby said. "By the way, I did a little preliminary look at the commercial real estate offerings in Hunter Springs."

"You did? Are we really considering this?"

"I'm only a partial owner," Ruby said. "This is mostly on you. But after the Hunter Springs mayor spoke to you like he did, I didn't think it would hurt to check into things."

"And what did you find?" Maggie asked. She was more interested in the idea of expansion than she was ready to admit.

"I found three really good possibilities," Ruby said. "Ironically, one of the properties is in an old gas station. It's part of the old downtown business district."

"A gas station?"

"Strange, right? But you should see the photos. It's really retro and spacious, and totally quirky," Ruby said.

They talked for a while about the other options and eventually Maggie knew she had to get home before she exploded with excitement at the idea of expansion.

CHAPTER SEVEN

It was well after dark when Bradley returned home from the fair in Hunter Springs. He said very little until he emerged from a hot shower and slumped into a chair in the living room.

"I don't know how you do that every day, Mom," he said. "That was a workout."

"The food truck is an animal all its own," Maggie conceded. "Did you enjoy it, though?"

A smile spread across his face. "I actually did," he said. "How did Wyatt do at Ruby's?"

"He played in the dirt," Maggie said with a broad grin. "When I got there, both of them looked like they had been taking dust baths. He was blissfully happy."

Bradley chuckled. "He's passed out in there," he

said. "Are you planning to open the food truck again in the morning?"

Maggie nodded. "I am. Ruby is training Naomi on the lunch prep this weekend," she said. "Do you want to come and hang out again?"

"I was thinking that we ought to be prepared to stay open as long as we were tonight, but that's a lot on one person," he said. "Some of the other vendors asked if they could stop by before the fair opens in the morning for some coffee and donuts."

"Huh, that's really neat," Maggie said. "We can do that."

Bradley sighed. "I suppose I ought to head for bed myself," he said.

"Is there something else going on, Bradley?" Maggie asked. "Did something happen at the food truck?"

"At the truck? No, not at all," he said. "But this whole thing with the tech firm in Joplin has me a little freaked out. I know what Brett said about not worrying so much about being a suspect, but the fact remains that the man I was supposed to meet with died and I am hanging on to the hope that a tiny receipt is going to prove that I had nothing to do with his death."

"I understand how upset you've got to be about all

of this, sweetheart," Maggie said. "But I don't think you have anything to worry about. Brett was pretty direct about that."

"Armored Shield called me back while I was working the food truck in Hunter Springs," Bradley admitted. "They want me to return for another interview. The man who called me, Mitch Leavy, was insistent that he meet with me. So much so that he was going to come and find me in Dogwood Mountain. He was strangely adamant."

"Are you worried about having another interview? Have you lost your nerve?" she asked.

Bradley yawned and shook his head. "It isn't that at all," he said. "I mean, part of me was frustrated because he interrupted my day in the food truck with the reality of my unemployment situation. But the phone call from Mitch has me unsettled. I feel like I'm being pulled into the spider's web."

"Whoa, that's very different from what I thought was going on here," Maggie said. "I didn't know that you were that concerned about this murder. You didn't even know William Anderson. You had no idea who he was. Heck, you never even met him in person. I don't think you have anything to worry about."

"It's less that I'm worried about the cops pulling me in now, although that is still bouncing around in my head. I'm more worried about the call from this man who wants, who insists, on meeting with me," he said. "You have to wonder, why is he so insistent?"

"Do you have a theory about why?" Maggie asked. She worked to understand what was eating away at her son.

"I don't, Mom," he said. "And that's the biggest part of the issue."

Maggie sighed. She felt the ache of the day in her back and her shoulders. "Do you want me to look into things for you?"

"Look into things like you've done before?" Bradley asked. He stared up at the ceiling. "Actually, Mom. I have no idea how you do the things you do and how you figure things out. But if you can come up with something, I think that would be wonderful."

Bradley rose and excused himself to the spare bedroom for the night. Maggie stood and headed to the kitchen to turn off the lights. She gazed outside through the back windows and surveyed the yard. Since her run-in with the man at the bookstore, she had the sinking feeling that someone might show up sneaking around her house again.

Maggie headed for her bedroom and closed the door behind her. She shivered at the thought of the vulnerability her son must be feeling. It was a feeling she had understood more times than she cared to admit herself.

Before she climbed into bed, she looked up the security firm on her phone. She scanned the company's website. William Anderson was still listed as the head of personnel. She looked through the rest of the site for any mention of Mitch Leavy. She yawned and glanced at the clock. Despite the later opening time at the fair, Maggie wanted to get a good night's sleep. She left the website on her phone and plugged it in for the night. The reminder would be the first thing she saw the following morning.

CHAPTER EIGHT

The fair was hopping the following morning. Maggie brewed coffee earlier than normal for the vendors that began to show up around eight. She'd started the mini donut machine at the same time and set out a dozen powdered sugar donuts as samples, then placed the first round of cinnamon rolls in the warming tray to raise.

By nine, the crowd had gathered outside of her windows. Maggie found herself flying between tasks and willing someone from the donut shop to swoop in and offer her a hand. At nine-thirty, Ruby called to check on her and report that Naomi had taken over the kitchen for the first time.

"I wish I had a way to count the crowds this

morning and compare it to yesterday," Maggie told her. "I swear this morning I've seen more people."

"More people," Ruby asked. "Maybe it's just a busier day, or the weather is nicer or something."

"More people at once, anyhow," Maggie said. "It's hard to explain, but there are never less than ten people lined up outside." She balanced the phone on her ear as she brewed another round of black coffee.

"Maybe I should book an appointment to see the old gas station in Hunter Springs." Ruby chuckled.

"You know what?" Maggie whispered. She collected another payment from a customer in between her comments. "I don't think that would be a bad idea."

"So, then, we really are considering expansion?"

"Well." Maggie turned away from the window. "I know this is impulsive and I should pay for months of studies to be done, but after what Mayor Huffy said, my gut instinct tells me that we should go for it."

"We have a lot to think about," Ruby said. "Staffing alone is going to take a lot of thought. But my gut tells me the same thing. Maybe we should sit down and think a little more about it before I call the realtor."

Maggie gazed over the people gathered in front of her food truck. She estimated twenty five to thirty people stood, waiting for a chance to order. "No, call the realtor," she said. "Call him and set something up. And while you're at it, send me some help! I'm drowning here!"

An hour later, Maggie was surprised by a knock on the door and a familiar face in the doorway.

"Morning, Mom," Bradley said. He stood in the doorway and smiled. "Need some help?"

"Actually, yes," she said. "You're here early. What do you want to do, and where is Wyatt?"

"Wyatt is hanging out with Orson and Brooks today," Bradley said. "And the question isn't what do I want to do, it's what do you want me to do?"

"Take over the order window," Maggie said. "I'll back you up."

"Works for me," Bradley said. He smiled at the next customer and took three new orders in a row.

"By the way, Jake will be along around noon to help me out. You're free to take off for a little while after that."

Maggie laughed heartily. "Did you just give me my walking papers, son?" she asked.

Bradley's face reddened. "I'm sorry." He blushed. "I guess I am used to giving out orders. Comes with being in the military."

"I guess so," Maggie said.

They worked together for a couple of hours before either of them got a break. Maggie smiled and welcomed Jake Jenkins into the food truck just before noon. Jake jumped right into the mix and helped with the lunch rush.

"Can you imagine if we had boxed lunches here?" Jake said when he passed by her.

"We might need a second food truck," Bradley said.

"Or an actual location," Maggie joked. She left the comment hanging and headed out for a short break. As soon as she was free, she decided to take out her phone and look at the security company's website once more. She walked down the main part of the fair until she found an empty picnic table and sat down. The website was filled with calls to action for security purposes. Maggie browsed around a little more until she found a word bubble next to a thumbnail picture of a man's head. The quote "call me for your small business security needs!" was followed by a "Mitch Leavy, salesman."

"Bingo!" Maggie clicked on the chat button and waited for a response.

"Hi! My name is Mitch! How can I help you?" A contact form appeared after the greeting. Maggie filled out her name and phone number. She left off her last name and hit the enter button. Almost immediately, she heard the ping indicating a text message. The automated message reassured her that the salesman would be in touch within twelve hours.

Maggie decided to keep her detective work from her son for the time being. She walked back up the main fair road and headed for The Taco Hut. She placed an order for three large walking tacos and three bottles of soda. While her food was being prepared, Maggie turned and watched the people pass by. She was delighted to see several groups carrying coffee cups or sacks with the Dogwood Donuts logo.

Her phone rang suddenly. Maggie checked the screen and cleared her throat. The number was unfamiliar, but she figured out that it might be Mitch Leavy. "Hello, this is Maggie," she said.

"Maggie? Mitch Leavy here. I'm with Cadence Guard," he said. "You left a message that you were interested in security for your small business?"

"I did," Maggie said. "I wanted a quote. How does that work?"

"For one, you tell me the name of your business and maybe your last name," Mitch said. He chuckled slightly. Maggie groaned inwardly.

"My goodness. I forgot to tell you the name of my business. It's Dogwood Donuts. I am actually looking at a second location as well," she said. She thought about her last name. She didn't want to tip the man off. "My name is Maggie Hollen." She chose her mother's maiden name rather than her own.

"Alright, ma'am? Is it Mrs. or Ms.?"

"Ms, but does that matter?"

"Oh, not at all," Mitch said. "But let's be straight with each other, okay? If I'm dealing with a man, I have a different security approach than I would with you, for example. Does that make sense? And if you're not married, that changes things even more. It's about statistics, right? Women are more vulnerable to different types of violent crimes than men are. I take that into consideration when I design a new security program."

"Okay, well," Maggie began. She was immediately put off by the emphasis on her gender. "What happens next?"

"First, you let me come out and take a look at the building itself," Mitch said. "And then I have a meeting with your local police department and get a picture of the crime in the area. And then we talk specifics and a budget."

"Speaking of budget, can you give me an idea of what we're looking at here? Am I going to need a second mortgage?"

"Ha! That's a really great line," Mitch said. "I hope you don't mind if I use that myself. Anyway, what's a good time for me to meet you? I am available this afternoon around three."

"I'm at a fair in Hunter Springs right now, and I won't be back in Dogwood Mountain until closer to five," she said. "How about five-thirty? The business closes at three."

"But you're in another town right now?"

"I have a food truck as well as the brick and mortar building," Maggie said.

"Well, a food truck adds to the security needs," he said. "I wish you had mentioned that already."

"I didn't because I'm more concerned about the physical location," Maggie said.

"Well, we'll talk about all of that later," Mitch said. Maggie rolled her eyes again. "Okay. I have the address here. Let's meet at five-thirty. I'll have to go into the building itself and take a good look around."

Maggie agreed to the meeting and hung up the phone just as her order was ready. She balanced the food in her hands and shoved the plastic coke bottles into her pockets. She knocked slightly at the door when she arrived at the back of the food truck. Jake opened the door and moved out of the way.

"I've got lunch," she said and smiled. She handed

the drinks off to the boys and settled into the chair herself.

"You go on and eat, Mom," Bradley said. "I'll keep working the window and then I'll eat my lunch when you take over again."

"You're doing it again," Maggie said.

"Doing what?"

"You're barking orders," she said. "It's hilarious."

"I keep doing that," Bradley said. "I'm so sorry, Mom."

Maggie looked out at the crowd and spotted Ruby waving at her. "Who knows, Bradley," she said. "Maybe you'll be in charge in one way or another after all."

CHAPTER NINE

Maggie stepped out of the truck and met Ruby just outside of the back door. "Did you see the gas station? Have you met with the real estate agent?"

Ruby nodded. "Don't you want to go inside?" she asked and nodded toward Jake, who was standing there looking at them with the door open to the truck.

"No, I wanted to talk to you outside for a second," Maggie said. She told Jake she'd be back in soon and sent him on his way, hoping he hadn't heard what she'd said. "You should see Bradley in there. He's in complete control. He forgets that he isn't back in the Navy, and he barks orders. Only it's not mean or overbearing. He just knows what to do now, so he organizes everyone else to do what they need to do."

"That's actually better than just funny," Ruby

61

said. "He shows that he can adapt to anything and take control."

Maggie nodded. "I know what you're thinking, and I've had the same thoughts. But I don't know that Bradley wants to come work for me."

"Maybe he won't be working for you directly," Ruby pointed out. "Maybe he could open a new location and be the boss of it. You'll still be the owner, but who owns this when you retire, anyway? I know that's a long time in the future yet, but it will most likely be Bradley."

Maggie shook her head. "I feel like we're getting ahead of ourselves," she said. "We don't even have a second location."

Ruby smiled and leaned her head to the side. "About that... I actually did see the gas station, Maggie. It's an adorable and whimsical space. It was actually more than a gas station. It was a four-car repair garage as well."

"And it's whimsical?"

"There was a craft store inside it last," Ruby said. "It hasn't been a gas station for at least five years."

"Oh, okay," Maggie said. "But what about the price? Surely there is a market for a property like that."

"The truth is, we could buy it outright," Ruby said. "Cash on the barrel."

"And there is no demand for it?"

"Ian, the agent, told me that the problem is that the property is quite a unique case and in a town this size, it is hard to find a fit. The gas station components were removed some time ago, so it isn't really cost effective for someone to try to reopen a gas station or a car repair place," Ruby said.

"Okay, that's a lot to think about. We can just pay cash for it. Are you sure?"

"More than," Ruby said, handing over a stack of paperwork for Maggie to look at.

She opened the folder and shook her head again. "I hope we're not being impulsive."

"Let's just see how the rest of the weekend goes and we can talk to Bradley afterwards," Ruby suggested.

"He might not even want to be a part of it," Maggie said. "I know he's worried about this situation with the man who wound up dead."

"Do you even know how the guy died?"

"No, and that's the other reason I wanted to talk to you out here first," Maggie said. "I did something."

"What did you do?" Ruby asked. "Why do I feel like Ricky asking Lucy what she did at the club?"

"Great reference." Maggie laughed. "And slightly appropriate. What I did was set up a consultation tonight at the donut shop with this guy who called Bradley."

"Wait," Ruby said. "I'm going to need more information than that."

Maggie sighed. "Okay. You know how the man he was set to have an interview with passed away, right?"

Ruby nodded. "Well, another man who represents the same company reached out to Bradley and really pushed setting up another meeting. He is suspicious about that."

"Well, business does go on," Ruby said. "Or is there something more to it?"

"I don't know what specifically has him upset, but he said he feels like he is being pulled into the spider's web," Maggie said. "This guy from the company, Mitch is his name, has pursued Bradley. He was even going to drive out to Dogwood Mountain to meet with him."

"Okay, so what did you do?"

"I went on the company website and found his contact information, and then proceeded to give him a fake last name and set up a security check up for the donut shop," Maggie said. She found herself practically beaming at her ingenuity.

Ruby dropped her head and sighed deeply. "You do realize how absolutely dangerous that is," she said.

Maggie nodded emphatically. "I wasn't going to do it without telling you and maybe Brett," she said.

"He's supposed to meet me tonight at five-thirty."

"Okay, and what is it you expect to find out?" Ruby asked.

"I already found out one thing," Maggie said. "The company Bradley was supposed to interview with was called Armored Shield. When he called me, he said the name was Cadence Guard."

"Okay," Ruby said. "That is weird. But I still don't know what you're hoping to accomplish with this."

"I hope I can determine if this Mitch Leavy guy is legitimate," Maggie said. "I'm afraid he's trying to lure my son into his web so he can somehow, someway pin the other guys murder on him. Or at least pin it close enough to him to cast suspicion."

"Why would he do that?"

"Well, if this guy had anything to do with it, he might be looking for a scapegoat," Maggie said. "And I refuse to let that be my son."

CHAPTER TEN

Jake stuck around and helped Bradley run the food truck for the remainder of the afternoon. Maggie promised to return that evening if business remained as active as it had the day before, but she had the feeling her son wouldn't reach out to her for help unless it was to pick the baby up.

She drove through town to head back to Dogwood Mountain and thought about what Ruby had told her outside of the food truck. Before she made it to the highway, she decided to turn back around and check out the property for herself.

Ruby's words bounced around in her head. They could afford to buy the property outright, and she saw the papers to prove it. She pulled off of the road for a second and double checked the real estate website for the property address. While she had a general idea of the location, she wanted to make sure she knew exactly where she was going.

When she pulled in front of the garage, she was struck by the size of the place. The building was about two-thirds garage and one-third a lobby area. Each of the garage doors had a full window overhead door, giving the place even more of a spacious look. Immediately, Maggie pictured an industrial aesthetic.

She parked her car close to the front of the building and got out. She walked close to the building but didn't want to get too close and set off the suspicions of any onlookers. But she stood close enough that she could see inside the lobby. It was roomy enough for a large kitchen. A wall separated the front lobby from another space in the back. Maggie pulled out her phone and immediately called Ruby.

"How much would it cost to install a kitchen in that place?" Maggie asked her. "The garage, I mean."

"I figured that's what you were talking about. I take it you drove by," Ruby said. "So, if you are there now, I assume you're looking at the lobby, correct?"

"I'm doing that exactly," Maggie agreed.

"Okay, so do you see the door in the wall dividing the front of the building from the back?"

"Yes, I see it."

"Pay attention to where that wall comes when you look out into the garage bays. That's how deep the back room is. And that entire back room is a kitchen."

"This place already has a kitchen in it? Why didn't you tell me about that earlier?"

"Probably because I was already a little too focused on the fact that you were planning to play Nancy Drew with this guy from the security company," Ruby said.

"Alright, fine," Maggie said. "I can't stop thinking about this place. Can you imagine black metal pipes and stainless steel counters?"

"And the garage doors have to stay," Ruby said.

"Absolutely," Maggie said. "I think we make this an industrial looking space but balance it with bright colors."

"A couple of warmer tones, like brown, maybe red, and a bright blue. Turquoise," Ruby added.

"I feel like we should just call the realtor," Maggie said with a long sigh.

"And do what? Put down a nonrefundable amount for earnest money? You don't think that would be a little irresponsible, do you?"

"That's an oddly specific question, but no, not really," Maggie replied.

"Good, because I wrote the realtor a check out of my own account," Ruby said. "I didn't want to pressure you, but I couldn't stop thinking about Bradley running a new donut shop there."

"Neither can I, to be honest with you," Maggie admitted. "Okay. I have to head to the donut shop. I have some work to do before I meet with Mitch Leavy. But that's just so awesome, Ruby. I can't believe you did that."

"Let's just say I had a vision of the future, and it was in Hunter Springs, too," Ruby said.

Maggie headed back to Dogwood Mountain and drove straight to the donut shop. She went to work right away on the cinnamon roll dough for the food truck for the following day. She was halfway through the scones when she glanced at the clock and had a momentary panic. It was already ten after five. Her plan had been to prepare a little bit more before Mitch Leavy showed up to assess her business for security needs.

What sort of security measures he offered, she still wasn't sure. She hadn't taken the time to look that closely into the services offered, but knew the limited equipment she currently had was enough to make him see it was possible she really needed his services. She glanced at the time again. Ten minutes after five. She placed the last batch of dough into a plastic tote and walked it into the cooler for the food truck the following morning.

Two minutes later, she had the baker's table cleared of excess flour. She returned to the sink and rinsed a clean rag in the hot, soapy water and turned back to clean and wipe the surface of the table. Ruby should be along soon.

But when she turned back, she stood nearly face to face with a strange man. He had come out of the clear blue and silently moved directly behind her.

"Oh! Who are you?" Maggie screamed and grabbed for the only weapon within her reach. She plunged her hand into the hot water and pulled out a long pair of tongs. She used the tongs to flip donuts in the deep fryer.

"Are you scared?" The man calmly walked around in a circle in the middle of the kitchen. "Are you terrified yet?"

"You are trespassing! Who are you?" Maggie shouted again. She held the edge of the tongs in front of her.

"Your plan is to defend yourself with a pair of tongs? Is this the grand plan?" he asked.

Maggie forced herself to take a deep breath and studied his face. Something sparked in her head. "You better not be that guy from the security company," she said.

The man pulled a business card from his wallet and offered it to Maggie. "That's exactly who I am," he said with a smug grin. "And I was able to walk right inside here and surprise you in a compromising position."

"You were supposed to be here twenty minutes from now, and you do not have permission to be inside this building without being invited inside! I don't know what sort of scam you are running here, but this is not the right way to win business," Maggie shouted.

"Well, I think you need to leave that to me, seeing as how I am the security professional and all," he said. "And this is a very effective method for getting business, especially from single women."

"By terrorizing them?"

"By showing them what's possible," he said. "Now, the first thing we're going to do is to remove these outdated security cameras and replace them with my own state-of-the-art computer monitored system. The next thing we're going to do is wire this place from bow to stern with a remote alarm system. My company will monitor the comings and goings daily. You and your employees will be issued key cards with limited access."

"Hold on, Mr. Leavy," Maggie broke in. "For one, I have not said one thing about ordering any of these services from your company. As a matter of fact, I am asking you to leave."

"Settle down and listen to me for a moment," he said. "You are failing to see the bigger picture. You are vulnerable here. And the way you are talking to me proves it."

"Mr. Leavy," Maggie said slowly. "I don't think you understand what I am telling you. I don't think I want to do business with someone who is going to break into my shop just to try to prove a point about how vulnerable I am to intruders. I think you need to leave."

"I told you I'm not going to do that. I am not going to leave here until you take advantage of the services I'm offering and protect yourself better," Mitch said.

"Maggie? Are you in there?" Ruby called out from the dining room. "The front door is standing wide open. Oh." She stopped when she spotted the strange man standing in front of Maggie and the tongs Maggie still held out in front of her.

"Who are you?" Mitch asked sternly.

"Why don't you answer your own question first," Ruby said flatly.

CHAPTER ELEVEN

Ruby stood with her arms folded across her chest. She glared hard at the man with the dozen or so leaflets spread out on the baker's table.

"You're representing a security company and you use a gotcha trick to try and scare female business owners into buying your services," Ruby said. "Is that what I understand here?"

Mitch waved his hands in the air. "You just don't get it," he said. He walked around in another circle. "This is why doing business with men is so much simpler." The last part he spoke more to himself.

"Then let me try to get it," Ruby continued. "You're sort of like a water filter salesman who brings a glass of sewer water to the customer's home to prove how filthy their water is."

"That's just disgusting," Mitch said. "You both need massive locks on the front and back doors. You need to upgrade to my systems. I have my tool kit in my truck, and I'll begin with installing a new alarm system. Installed tonight, but I prefer to work alone. So, if you two can finish up here, I'll get started."

"You have some audacity," Ruby said. "I'll give you that."

"Tell me about this potential new location," Mitch continued. "And this food truck. I didn't see it outside. But I did see another one parked up there close to the sign. That one is hopping with business. I assume that truck isn't owned by you, Ms. Sharpe."

"Stop," Maggie said at last. "I think you need to leave. I've made it plain and clear that I don't want your services."

Mitch shook his head again and stared at the floor. "Maybe you don't know salesmen like me," he said. "But I don't take no for an answer. You might as well get out of here and let me get busy with what I need to do. Because I will be installing that alarm system before I leave here. I can guarantee that."

"I'm done with this nonsense," Ruby said. She pulled her phone out of her pocket. "I think I'll give Brett a call."

"Who's Brett?"

"Brett Mission is the chief of police and her boyfriend," Ruby said. She nodded at Maggie.

"Whoa," Mitch said. "First, there is no reason to call the police. And second, you said you were single."

"I said I wasn't married," Maggie said. She turned to Ruby. "Call him. Do it now."

Ruby turned toward the deep fryer and began dialing.

"Fine, fine," Mitch said. He threw his hands above his head. He gathered up his pamphlets and shoved them at Maggie as he passed her. "I will be back. You can bet on that." He winked and nodded in her direction, then stalked loudly through the swinging door and headed out the front. Maggie followed behind him and closed and locked the door behind him. Ruby followed quickly behind.

"I hope you really did call Brett," Maggie said. "I have a feeling this is going to be an important thing to share with him."

Brett arrived a few moments later. Maggie invited him into the office to look over the footage from the security cameras she did have installed. She watched over his shoulder for the first time and watched as the man broke into the front door of her business.

"That makes me so mad," Maggie said. "What sort of a company uses such tactics?"

"None I've ever heard of," Brett said. "I'm going to head back to the office and prepare this as evidence and send it to the Joplin police." He stood and removed the flash drive from Maggie's laptop.

"And I think we'll call the locksmith and have that lock changed yet again," Ruby said.

"We might as well put him on notice for Hunter Springs," Ruby said. "We'll need his services there, too."

"You don't think we ought to use a locksmith from Hunter Springs? That might not bode well for a new business there," Maggie said.

"I think the locksmith serves both communities," Ruby said.

"Hold on," Brett said as they were talking. "What's going on in Hunter Springs? You can't move the donut shop there."

Ruby glanced at Maggie and winked. "Nothing is settled yet, so keep this under your hat," she said. "But there's a strong chance of a second location in Hunter Springs."

"What? Where?" he asked.

"Do you remember the old filling station downtown?"

Brett nodded. "I thought they converted that into an antique store or something," he said.

"They did, but the place is for sale again," Ruby explained.

"And who will be running a second location?"

"We'll figure that out later," Maggie said. "And it isn't a sure thing."

"Which is why you want me to keep it under my hat." Brett smiled.

"Just for now," Ruby said.

"Just until you have time to speak to Bradley about it too, right?" Brett winked at Maggie and headed for his car.

"I'm going home now," Maggie announced after they watched Brett's car head out of the donut shop parking lot.

"And are you going to sleep, or do you plan to do a little more looking into things?" Ruby asked.

Maggie nodded. "I plan to check out the company again," she said. "I'm going to contact another sales representative and ask about these tactics."

"Good thing I brought my laptop in the truck with me," Ruby grinned. "I'm coming over."

CHAPTER TWELVE

Maggie placed two tea bags into mugs and poured hot water over the top. "I think it would be better if I used my name this time," Ruby announced from the table. "I won't use Cobb, though."

"What are you going to use?"

"What did you use?

"My mother's maiden name," Maggie said and smiled.

"McGillicutty, it is," Ruby said. She began typing on the keyboard and waited. A second later, her cell phone rang. She placed the phone on the table in front of her and turned on the speaker. "Hello?"

"Hi, Mrs. McGillicutty? My name is Rachel Ada and I am with Armored Shield Security. I think you just filled out a request for information?"

"That was fast," Ruby said. "Do you always call that fast?"

"It is part of our company policy to call within two hours of receiving a notification," Rachel said.

"Okay, well, I just had a couple of questions about security around my house," Ruby said and shrugged.

She was doing her best to wing it on the phone. She glanced at Maggie as she spoke. "I have a large home out in the country about an hour from Joplin. Do you serve that far?"

"Not usually," the woman said.

Maggie hurriedly wrote out a question on a piece of paper and slid it over to Ruby. 'Ask about another company they give their business to? Maybe Cadence Guard?'

Ruby nodded. "Do you have another company you hand your referrals off to out this way? Or another company you would recommend?"

"Um, not especially," Rachel said over the phone. "We don't usually go that far south, but I can look into another recommendation for you. Maybe out of Fayetteville."

Maggie tapped the paper in front of her again. "Ma'am, can you tell me about a company called Cadence Guard?"

There was an audible sigh over the phone. "Who is this? Is this some sort of a joke?"

"No, no," Ruby said quickly. "I can assure you that it isn't."

"Then why are you asking me about that company?" Rachel asked. She practically whispered the question.

"Because a friend of mine contacted your company just as I did and the guy showed up at her business that same day," Ruby said. "He broke into her business and scared her to death just to prove that she needed your company's services."

"Wait, he did what? I think you have confused this company with another one," she said. "We do not break into people's homes or businesses to drum up business."

"This guy did, and this guy was on your website and used the same contact form to contact her," Ruby said.

"Are you sure? Maybe you should have your friend contact me in person," Rachel said.

"She's sitting right here, Ms. Ada," Maggie said. "And this isn't a gotcha call. I promise that. I was just curious to see if this was a company tactic. And if it was, I planned to contact the Missouri Attorney General's Office in the morning."

"Oh, it absolutely isn't something we do here," Rachel said. "Who was this person you dealt with? Can you give me a name, or at least a description? We've had some changes in personnel lately. Unfortunately, one of our coworkers was also killed. But we have no idea if that was associated with his personal life or his work."

"The man's name was Mitch Leavy," Maggie began. "And he was so fast talking and so insistent that he refused to take no for an answer-"

"What name did you say again?" Rachel interrupted her to ask.

"Mitch Leavy," Maggie replied.

"Ladies, Mitch Leavy is not a part of this company any longer. He was let go over three months ago."

"His photo is still on your website," Ruby said.

"We are pretty slow to update our online presence, but he was fired back in May. He's not supposed to have any access to our lead generation software. That's the contact form you filled out earlier, Mrs. McGillicutty."

"It's actually Cobb," Ruby said. "But go on. Why was Leavy fired?"

"You know I can't go into that," Rachel said. "But let me just tell you this: If Mitch Leavy was in your business this afternoon, I sure hope you called a lock-smith when he left."

"Ms. Ada," Ruby asked slowly. "Your company recently suffered a loss. Is it possible that we need to inform a police officer about Mitch Leavy's behavior?"

"Are you two reporters or something?" Rachel snapped. "Because I think you're supposed to reveal that before you interview someone. Are you recording me?"

"Of course, we're not recording you," Ruby said. "And no, we are not reporters."

"Okay, well, I guess I believe you," Rachel said. "But this is a weird conversation."

"I agree," Maggie said. "I think we've taken up enough of your time."

Ruby nodded and disconnected the call. "I wondered if you were going to talk about Bradley."

"I thought about it," Maggie said. "But I don't want to mention his name and somehow have it come back on him."

CHAPTER THIRTEEN

Sunday morning was the final morning of the fair in Hunter Springs. Once again, Bradley arranged for childcare for Wyatt while he manned the food truck. Maggie promised to show up later in the morning. The story she'd told her son was that she wanted to sleep in for once, but the truth was that she had set up a meeting with the real estate agent to tour the gas station in Hunter Springs for herself.

Ruby drove separately to meet her there. Maggie wasn't sure what she planned to do, but she figured she had to at least meet with the realtor or live with regret.

"This is huge," Maggie said when she walked through the lobby side.

"Wait until you see the kitchen," Ruby said.

Maggie followed the realtor through the door and into the large space. It was entirely open. Aside from a small employee restroom and a double cooler. "It's practically cavernous," she said.

"It's already got a deep fryer that will work and triple sinks," Ruby said. "We can add one of the donut machines here if we choose. And we'll need a glazer."

"And some place to store everything," Maggie said. She pointed to the back corner near the cooler. "Right there. Metal shelving across the back wall and up the side."

"There's a storage shed out back with a few things left inside that comes with the place. It's temperature controlled, too." The agent pointed to the door at the rear of the kitchen.

"Let's have a look-see," Ruby said. "If you can let us in."

The realtor nodded his head and led them out into the alley behind the old station. He unlocked the large shed and flipped on the light switch. "Look," Maggie gasped. Stacks of black, white, and red tables lined the back, along with matching chairs. "It has sort of a retro vibe."

"That it does," the agent agreed. "Look over

there." Maggie and Ruby followed him to the far right.

"We won't have to buy metal shelving after all," Maggie said. She counted four free-standing units, as many as she had at the location back in Dogwood Mountain.

"This place is as close to turnkey as we can get within our budget," Ruby said.

The realtor sighed. "I hope you all decide what you want to do fairly quickly," he said. "I have another client wanting to look at this place. And I'll admit, the seller is eager to be rid of this place."

"Do you have an appointment set up?" Maggie asked.

The realtor shook his head. "Not yet. I've been putting them off," he said. "She wants to open a doll museum here. No one wants a doll museum. But if you all open a donut shop? Well, that will immediately increase property values across the board."

"Maggie?" Ruby asked with an exaggerated shrug of her shoulders.

"I think you better break the news to your other client." Maggie smiled. "This property is no longer for sale."

"Yes! I'm so glad," Ruby said and fist-pumped

the air. The realtor took off to make a call, leaving them alone to talk.

"Now let's hope my son wants to work here," Maggie said. "Otherwise, we're going to be running ourselves crazy trying to cover both places."

After the final walk-through, Ruby headed back to Dogwood Mountain with the task of drawing up a business plan. Maggie had a bigger concern. She needed to approach the idea with her son and determine whether the decision to jump in with both feet had been a hasty one.

"We have time to set things up before we close on the property," Ruby advised her. "After that, we'll need some serious revenue coming from Hunter Springs."

"I think we ought to leave the food truck here in the beginning," Maggie suggested. "Park it at the gas station with a sign that says 'Coming Soon' or something like that."

"That's an excellent idea," Ruby said with a smile. "In the meantime, why don't you bring Bradley by here after you shut things down for the night?"

Maggie nodded and headed for the front gate to the fair immediately after she watched Ruby drive in the other direction. It was just after ten when she walked down the main part of the fair and headed for the food truck. Although there were still plenty of people around, the crowd seemed more laid back and relaxed.

"Morning," she said to Bradley when she stepped up inside the truck. "How are things going?"

She dodged out of Jake's way and huddled in the corner near the refrigerator.

"Fine, Mom," Bradley said from the front window. "Jake, two more cinnamon rolls."

"On it," Jake said. He twirled around Maggie and produced two warmed cinnamon rolls in to-go boxes.

"You guys have sort of a rhythm worked out here," she said. She was more impressed than she could explain. Jake had always been hard working, but here he seemed to shine.

Maggie went to work refilling the coffee maker and mixing more batter for the mini donut machine. She continued to work in the background while Jake and Bradley ran the front. When she had a moment, she pulled out her phone and texted Ruby.

"I think I might have figured out who Bradley should take with him to Hunter Springs," she wrote, and snapped a photo of the pair working together.

"That's a long way for Jake to drive," Ruby replied. "But that will be up to them to work out, I guess."

Maggie shoved her phone back into her pocket. She prepared a cup of coffee for herself and placed one hand on Jake's shoulder. The crowd had thinned for a moment. "Why don't you run out and catch a short break," she said. "I can help Bradley out if things get too crazy."

"Are you sure?" Jake asked. "I'd like to look around a bit. This town is bigger than Dogwood Mountain." His eyes drifted toward a group of young women walking slowly past.

"I'm absolutely sure," she said and laughed when he rushed out after the group of women.

"Doesn't take much to keep him happy," she said to her son when Jake had gone.

"Not much, and he's a really hard worker, Mom," Bradley said. "I think you lucked out with him."

"I've been pretty lucky with all of our staff members, especially the ones who have become family."

"Like Ruby, Orson, and Myra?"

"Especially them." Maggie smiled.

"There are a couple of things I wanted to talk over with you, while we have a second," Maggie said. She wanted to fill him in on what she had discovered about Mitch before she started in about the new location. "I had a run in with a man from the security company you wanted to work at, Mitch Leavy. He came to the donut shop last night. In fact, he broke in the front door just to prove to me that I need his services."

"What? He did that?" Bradley said. His voice raised. "Did you call Brett? Was he arrested?"

"Brett knows all about it, and Ruby arrived before things went too far, but that guy doesn't believe in taking no for an answer."

"Tell me about it," Bradley said. "He's left four more messages just since last night."

"There's a little more to the story," Maggie said. She filled him in on the phone call with Rachel Ada from the actual company.

"Wait, wait," Bradley said. "I am so confused. Mitch doesn't work for the same company I had an interview for?"

"She said Leavy had been fired from Armored Shield three months ago," Maggie said. "Somehow, he still has access to the company's website. Or he did. I have a feeling that changed the second we got off of the phone last night."

"I wonder if they have figured out who killed William Anderson?" Bradley asked. "Maybe I dodged a bullet not working for that company."

"That's an interesting choice of words," Maggie

said. "And maybe you're right." She inhaled deeply and prepared to ask him about his future plans.

"You know, Mom," Bradley said before she could form a new sentence. "This weekend really has me thinking about things."

"What things?" she asked. A woman stepped up to the order window and asked for a dozen mini donuts and a vanilla latte.

"Well, for one thing, what I want to do with my life," he said when the woman stepped away.

"I thought you wanted to get a job in Joplin so you can live close by," Maggie said. "Or has that changed?"

"The living close by hasn't changed," Bradley said. Maggie exhaled a long sigh of relief. "But the job in Joplin has. I know it might be asking a lot, but is there a possibility that you have a position for me at the donut shop? I know that seems so stupid, but I can't tell you how much I've enjoyed working here. Maybe that's it. Maybe I can keep the food truck here for a few weeks. The response is good so far. I bet we could make more than enough money to justify my salary."

"Bradley," Maggie said when her son stopped for a breath. "That's something I wanted to talk to you about."

"I think I can do it all by myself, Mom. And you don't have to pay me much. Just enough to earn my keep at your house and to pay for someone to watch Wyatt."

"Bradley," she cut in. She was about to lay it all out for him, the second location, and the fact that she had already purchased it, when she spotted a familiar face in front of the food truck.

"What, Mom?"

"Does Mitch know what you look like?" she asked. Leavy stood just over ten feet away. His eyes were fixed on the two of them, though Maggie was sure he hadn't noticed them looking back.

"He should," Bradley said. "I sent a video application to the entire company. He mentioned it in one of the messages he left for me. But that makes no sense if he was fired so long ago…"

"That's not good," she said and pointed out the front window. "None of it is."

"Is that him staring at us?" Bradley asked quietly.

"I'm afraid it is," Maggie said.

CHAPTER FOURTEEN

As soon as he had appeared in front of the food truck, Mitch Leavy disappeared from her view. The crowd swelled around where he stood. Maggie lost track of him, but she was sure that he had seen her and her son. Given the huge lettering on the front and sides of the food truck, it was clear that the food truck belonged to the Dogwood Donut shop.

"What do you think we ought to do?" Bradley asked.

"I think we might need to call Brett and ask for his advice," Maggie said. "We might want to have Brooks keep an extra eye on the donut shop back home, too."

"I wish Jake would get back here," Bradley said.

"That way, we could leave him here while you and I split up and go looking for Mitch."

"What would you do if you found him?" Maggie asked her son.

He sighed. "I don't really know, Mom. But I sure want to talk to him about his behavior toward you."

Maggie turned to the order window and continued to work. Bradley took over running and preparing the orders while she worked. A new rush of people began to approach, many of them dressed in their church clothes. Maggie and Bradley worked nonstop for over an hour before it dawned on her that Jake had not returned.

"I think we need to go and look for Jake," she said to her son when there was a break in the crowd. "He isn't answering his cell phone."

"What about the food truck?" Bradley asked her.

"We're just going to close it down." Maggie shut the order windows and pushed the "Sorry, We're Closed" sign in the front window. They stepped out and locked the door behind them. Maggie headed straight down the main road. Bradley went the other way. As soon as she was out of sight, Maggie's phone rang.

"Okay, Mom," Bradley said as he walked. "I just left the bathroom area, and he's not there."

"I don't see him in the vendor booths up here, either," Maggie said. "I think I'll head down toward the other end next."

"And I'll go toward the midway," Bradley said.

Maggie remained on the phone with her son as she continued to walk up and down the roads through the fair. She could hear him breathe as he walked, but they said nothing as they searched for Jake. After their first pass through, Maggie suggested that they try one more time and then meet back at the food truck just to make sure Jake hadn't missed them and headed back there himself.

"It's been thirty minutes," Maggie said when she passed The Taco Hut for the third time. "I'm going back to the food truck right now."

"I can see it right now," Bradley said. "I'll meet you there in a second."

Maggie hung up the phone with her son at last and dialed Ruby immediately. "Have you heard from Jake?" she asked before she could even say "hello."

"Jake? No," Ruby said. "Should I have heard from him? I thought he was at the fair with the two of you."

"He was," Maggie said quickly. "But I sent him on a break. And then I saw Mitch Leavy staring at Bradley and me from outside the food truck. Now we can't find him. He's not answering his cell phone."

"I take it you have been looking for him?" Ruby asked.

"We shut down the truck and split up," Maggie said. "That was half an hour ago. And I'm just walking back up to the food truck to meet up with Bradley again."

"He's not here," Bradley said when she approached.

"Find security and report him missing," Ruby directed. "I'm going to hang up with you and call Brett. He has enough background in this story and I think he will do a better job reporting this to the police."

Maggie agreed and hung up the phone. Bradley volunteered to stay with the food truck in case Jake reappeared while Maggie continued to walk around looking for him.

"Are you guys about to open back up?" a middle-aged woman in a floral dress asked when they unlocked the back door.

"I'm sorry," Maggie said. "One of our employees has gone missing and we're a little distracted trying to find him."

"Oh, that's too bad," the woman said. "About

your employee, too. We sure love your donut shop, and this is the last day of the fair and all."

"Don't worry," Maggie called back out to the woman. "We'll be back with the truck next weekend."

"We will?" Bradley asked.

"Where at?" A man dressed in a suit next to the woman in the dress asked.

"At the old gas station downtown," Maggie said. "We're opening up a second location there very soon."

"You are? That's great!"

"We are," Maggie said. "I'm sorry. We have to find our worker. Please watch the newspaper for the opening."

"And if you see this young man, please let the police know," Bradley said. He held up his phone. Jake's photo was on the screen.

"I should have done that," Maggie said when they were alone again.

"What's this about a new location?" Bradley asked.

"Later," Maggie said. "Right now, we need to concentrate on finding Jake." Bradley nodded and set his cell phone on the counter.

Maggie headed back outside and walked straight for the security shack. She spotted two county sheriff deputies when she approached the shack. "Excuse me," she said, loud enough for the security guard and the deputies to hear. "I have a missing employee. I need help."

One of the deputies turned around quickly and walked around the shack. "Are you the owner of the donut truck?"

"I am. Maggie Sharpe," she said quickly. "The young man's name is Jake Jenkins. He's about twenty years old and he left close to an hour ago on a break."

The deputy held up her hand. "The police chief from over in Dogwood Mountain called us already and filled us in on what was going on. He sent over a photo already."

"Okay, what do we do now?" Maggie asked.

"Right now, you head back to the food truck and wait for word from us."

"My son is there right now," Maggie said.

"Then if there is another place you think he might have gone, head there and call me if you find anything," she said. "I'm Deputy Thompson with the Sheriff's Department." She handed over a card with her number on it.

Maggie accepted the card and headed back to the food truck. "I have an idea," she announced to her son through the food window. She took out her phone and held the deputy's card up and snapped a photo with it. She left the card with her son with the instructions to call if Jake happened to come back.

Her phone rang before she made it out of the fair and to her car. "Mom, where are you going?" Bradley demanded. "You left without telling me."

"I'm going to drive around a little," she said.

"Okay, well, be careful."

"I will, and I'll be on the phone with Ruby the whole time I'm looking." She hung up the phone and called Ruby immediately and filled her in on what was happening.

Maggie put the call on speaker and placed the phone on the seat next to her. As she drove, her head was on a swivel. She turned into the downtown area and slowed down when she spotted the old filling station. She swore she saw movement inside.

"Ruby, do you think anyone would be at the old filling station right now? Like the realtor or owner or something?"

"Why?" Ruby asked. "What do you see? I'm on my way."

"I don't know, but I'm going to find out." Maggie parked her car on the side street and walked across the road to the parking lot. She stayed close to the side of the building. She peered inside the windows but saw nothing. She decided to move around the back of the building. She wanted to come up the other side without giving her presence away through the windows in the overhead doors.

She was just outside of the kitchen door in the back. She paused when she thought she heard something inside. The noise was faint, more like a scurrying sound than anything. But it made her stop and listen a moment longer. The next noise came several decibels louder and caused her to jump where she stood. She heard a loud clank of metal and then metal scraping across the floor. She ran to the back door and pulled hard on the handle, but the door wouldn't budge.

She heard shouting next. Although she couldn't make out the words, she could hear two loud male voices inside the kitchen. She ran to the other end of the building and came up the other side. She stopped on the corner and pulled her phone out and dialed the county deputy's number.

"Thompson," the deputy said when she answered.

"This is Maggie Sharpe. Do you know the old filling station downtown?" she asked as fast as she could speak.

"Yeah, why?"

"I'm there now. I can hear a scuffle inside. Men

yelling. Please hurry." She hung up the phone and rounded the corner. She peered inside the windows and saw nothing. Her phone rang again. She answered it without looking at the number on the front.

"Maggie?"

Maggie breathed hard for a moment. "Jake?" She was confused at the voice on the other end.

"Yeah, it's me," Jake said. "I was, um, without my phone for a little while. I don't know where I'm at, but I think it's still in Hunter Springs."

"Are you okay, Jake? Are you hurt?"

"Naw," Jake said. "My fists are a little raw."

"Did someone take you from the fair?"

"Yeah, there was this older guy. He had a gun. But I'm all good now," Jake said.

For a moment, Maggie stood still, too shocked to move. "Where is the man now?" she asked at last.

"He's locked in the cooler at this place," Jake said. "You won't believe it. It's like an old mechanic's garage, but with a kitchen."

CHAPTER FIFTEEN

The sheriff's deputy arrived first, followed quickly by Ruby and the realtor with the keys. Maggie followed the deputy inside, where Jake was seated on a black wooden bar stool watching the cooler door.

"He's in there," Jake told the deputy. "His gun is in the sink."

Maggie stood by Jake and watched as the deputy opened the cooler door and took Mitch Leavy into custody. He said nothing, but stared hard at her while Deputy Thompson wrestled him into handcuffs.

"I'm going to need your statement," the deputy said to Jake.

"I'll be right behind you," he said.

Deputy Thompson led Leavy out of the building.

Bradley rushed in. "What happened?" he asked Jake as soon as he entered.

"Depends on when you want me to start," Jake said. "After I left the food truck, I followed the girls down toward the picnic area. This one girl, Shannon, oh man, is she cute."

"Maybe start where you ran into trouble," Ruby said.

"Oh, okay," Jake said. He winked at Bradley. "I'll tell you all about Shannon later."

"Jake," Maggie warned.

"Okay, okay," Jake said. "Funny, you sound like my mom. And that's why that guy took me, I guess. He thought I was Bradley's little brother."

"Where did he grab you?" Ruby asked.

"I went to the porta-johns," Jake said. "When I tried to come back out into the fresh air, this guy was leaning on the door. He had a gun in his hand, and he jammed it into my side. I thought he was just going to mug me at first, but then he started asking me bizarre questions about you guys and something about a new location. He asked me if I heard anybody talking about places and I said something about a gas station because I heard you guys chatting about it." He nodded to Ruby and Maggie.

"Did he say why he took you?" Maggie asked.

Jake nodded. "Yeah, he said you ruined his chances to clear his name or something. I got the feeling he was trying to use Bradley to clear himself, although I don't know how."

"I think I do," Maggie said. "He was going to try to blame you for William Anderson's death somehow. It was going to be his ticket out of suspicion."

"I think he was going to give you something that belonged to some dead guy," Jake continued. "He said something about giving you something that belonged to a dead man."

"Mr. Jenkins," Deputy Thompson called out from the parking lot. "We need to get your statement."

"I guess I better run out there and get this over with. By the way," Jake said. "Is this really our new location?"

Maggie smiled and nodded her head. "It is. This is the home of the new Hunter Springs Donuts," she said. "Or something along those lines."

Jake looked around and gave her a double thumbs up. "Awesome," he said and headed outside to talk to the sheriff's deputies.

"I feel so bad," Bradley said. "He should have taken me."

"No, he should have been in jail already for the

109

murder of William Anderson," Ruby said. "This is not your fault. Not in any way, shape, or form."

"She's right," Maggie said. "If anything, it's my fault for meddling with the investigation."

"I don't think that's true," Brett said from the lobby doorway. "I think you might have been the one to break the case open." He walked across the kitchen and joined them in front of the cooler.

"How so?" Maggie asked him.

"I just spoke with the sheriff's main detective here," he said. "A woman named Rachel Ada called the Joplin Police this morning and reported her suspicions, who in turn contacted the county sheriff. She named Mitch Leavy as her former coworker who had made threats to not only herself, but William Anderson as well. I understand that Anderson fired Leavy from the company a few months back."

"That does make me feel better," Maggie said. "Rachel Ada was the woman Ruby and I spoke with last night."

Bradley walked toward the triple sink and stopped to look around. "So, is this it? Is this your new location?"

Maggie glanced at Ruby. "It is," she said. "What do you think?"

"I think it's massive," Bradley said. "And I think

EASY COME EASY DOUGH

it's going to be quite the place. It's actually sort of brilliant. Those garage doors can open up in the warmer months. We can really spread people out here and give the place sort of a coffee house vibe as well."

"You guys aren't leaving Dogwood Mountain, are you?" Brett asked.

"No, this is a second location," Ruby said quickly. "We're going to park the food truck here to start out while we remodel the inside."

"It shouldn't take much," Bradley cut in. He continued his walk around the large kitchen. "Are you going to put another automatic donut machine here?"

"I think so," Maggie said. "It sort of depends on the thoughts of the person we're going to hire to run this place."

"Wait, you're not going to run it yourself?" Brett asked, a look of relief coming over his face.

"No, I don't want to leave Dogwood Mountain. We're having someone take this place on and run with it," Maggie said. "Ruby has the city council to keep her busy."

"And my farm," Ruby added.

"So, who is going to run this place?" Brett asked.

"Depends," Maggie said. "Bradley?"

"Mom," Bradley said. His eyes filled immediately

with tears. "Are you seriously asking me to open a new location for your business? Here in Hunter Springs?"

Maggie smiled and shrugged. "If you are sure you don't want a job in tech," she said. She walked to her son and placed her arms around his shoulders. "You are the main reason we decided to jump in with both feet."

Bradley hugged her tightly for several moments.

"I don't think we heard whether or not you're going to accept the position," Ruby called from the other side of the room.

Bradley released his mother and looked around the room again. "I think I would be an idiot not to say yes," he said. "But I have one question."

"What's that?" Maggie asked.

"Can I take the kid with me?" He nodded toward Jake, who had just returned from outside. "Flo told me she has a prospect for a new employee, so I'm sure she wouldn't mind."

"Wait, where am I going?" Jake asked.

"Here, if you want to come and work for this guy," Ruby said, pointing at Bradley.

"Yup," Maggie agreed. "If it's okay with Flo, it's perfect for us."

Jake nodded and walked toward Bradley. He

answered with a high-five. The pair began to walk around the kitchen before they headed into the lobby, chatting along the way. Maggie returned to where the others stood.

"Does this mean you're going to be busier now with Jake gone?" Brett whispered in her ear. "Because I was going to ask you about a little getaway to the Smoky Mountains in a few weeks."

"I think I can carve out some time for something so important." She leaned into Brett and rested her head on his shoulder. Things were finally settling into place.

AUTHOR'S NOTE

I'd love to hear your thoughts on my books, the storylines, and anything else that you'd like to comment on—reader feedback is very important to me. My contact information, along with some other helpful links, is listed on the next page. If you'd like to be on my list of "folks to contact" with updates, release and sales notifications, etc.... just shoot me an email and let me know. Thanks for reading!

Also...

... if you're looking for more great reads, Summer Prescott Books publishes several popular series by outstanding Cozy Mystery authors.

CONTACT SUMMER PRESCOTT BOOKS PUBLISHING

Blog and Book Catalog: http://summerprescottbooks.com

Email: summer.prescott.cozies@gmail.com

And…be sure to check out the Summer Prescott Cozy Mysteries fan page and Summer Prescott Books Publishing Page on Facebook – let's be friends!

To sign up for our fun and exciting newsletter, which will give you opportunities to win prizes and swag, enter contests, and be the first to know about New Releases, click here: http://summerprescottbooks.com

Made in the USA
Columbia, SC
20 August 2022